LITTLE MISS TROUBLE

by Roger Hargreaves

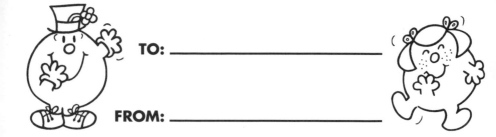

TO: _____

FROM: _____

LITTLE MISS TROUBLE

By Roger Hargreaves

Grosset & Dunlap
An Imprint of Penguin Random House

"Here comes trouble," people used to say.

And who do you think would come walking along?

That's right!

Little Miss Trouble.

Oh, the trouble she caused.

One morning she went to see Mr. Uppity.

"Do you know what Mr. Small calls you behind your back?" she asked him.

"No," replied Mr. Uppity. "What does Mr. Small call me behind my back?"

Little Miss Trouble looked at him.

"Fatty!" she said.

Now, Mr. Uppity didn't like that.

Not at all.

Not one little bit.

He went immediately to see Mr. Small.

"How dare you call me FATTY!?" he shouted.

"But . . ." stammered Mr. Small, who never had called him Fatty.

"But . . ."

"But nothing," shouted Mr. Uppity.

And he hit poor Mr. Small.

Ouch!

And gave him a black eye.

Poor Mr. Small.

Little Miss Trouble, who was hiding behind a tree, hugged herself with glee.

"Oh, I do so like making trouble," she giggled to herself.

Naughty girl!

Little Miss Trouble went to see Mr. Clever.

"Do you know what Mr. Small calls you behind your back?" she asked him.

"No," replied Mr. Clever. "Tell me! What does Mr. Small call me behind my back?"

Little Miss Trouble looked at him.

"Big Nose!" she said.

Now.

Mr. Clever didn't like that very much either.

Off he rushed.

And, when he found Mr. Small, without waiting for an explanation, he punched him!

Hard!

In the other eye!

Poor Mr. Small.

Two black eyes for something he'd never done.

"Oh look at you," Little Miss Trouble laughed when she saw him.

"It's all your fault," said Mr. Small.

"True," she said.

And walked off.

Poor Mr. Small had to go to the doctor.

"Good heavens!" exclaimed Doctor Makeyouwell when he saw him. "Whatever happened to you?"

Mr. Small explained.

"I think," Doctor Makeyouwell said when he'd heard what Mr. Small had to tell him, "that something should be done about that little lady! What she needs is . . ."

Then he stopped.

And he chuckled.

"That's it," he laughed.

"What's it?" asked Mr. Small.

And Doctor Makeyouwell whispered something to Mr. Small.

Would you like to know what he whispered?

Not telling you!

It's a secret!

That afternoon Mr. Small went to see Mr. Tickle.

"Do you know what Little Miss Trouble calls you behind your back?" he asked.

"No," said Mr. Tickle. "What does Little Miss Trouble call me behind my back?"

Mr. Small looked at him.

"Pudding Face!" he said.

Then Mr. Small went to see Mr. Bump.

"Do you know what Little Miss Trouble calls you behind your back?" he asked.

"No," said Mr. Bump. "What does Little Miss Trouble call me behind my back?"

Mr. Small looked at him.

"Mr. Nitwit!" he said.

Little Miss Trouble was in trouble.

"How dare you call me Pudding Face?!" cried Mr. Tickle.

And tickled her.

"And how dare you call me Mr. Nitwit?!" cried Mr. Bump.

And bumped her.

Now, I don't know whether you've ever been tickled and bumped at the same time, but it's not much fun.

In fact, it's no fun at all.

Ticklebumpticklebumpticklebumpticklebump!

For ten minutes.

And ten minutes of ticklebumping is a long time.

I can tell you!

Later that evening Doctor Makeyouwell strolled around to see Mr. Small.

"How are the eyes?" he asked.

"Oh much better now thank you," replied Mr. Small.

"And did our little plan work?" asked the doctor.

"It did indeed," grinned Mr. Small.

"Shake," said Doctor Makeyouwell.

And they shook hands.

Well.

Not quite hands.

Doctor Makeyouwell then strolled over to see Little Miss Trouble.

She was feeling very sorry for herself.

"What's wrong with you?" he asked her.

And she told him all about it.

All about everything.

Doctor Makeyouwell looked at her.

"Cheer up," he said. "You know what you've just had, don't you?"

Little Miss Trouble shook her head.

"A taste of your own medicine," he chuckled.

And went home.

For supper.

MR. MEN   LITTLE MISS
by Roger Hargreaves

SIL-5018

GROSSET & DUNLAP
Penguin Young Readers Group
An Imprint of Penguin Random House LLC

ISBN 9780843174267   14 13 12 11 10

Little Miss
Bossy

Little Miss
Naughty

Little Miss
Neat

Little Miss
Sunshine

Little Miss
Tiny

Little Miss
Trouble

Little Miss
Giggles

Little Miss
Helpful

Little Miss
Magic

Little Miss
Shy

Little Miss
Splendid

Little Miss
Twins

Little Miss
Chatterbox

Little Miss
Ditzy

Little Miss
Late

Little Miss
Lucky

Little Miss
Scatterbrain

Little Miss
Star

Little Miss
Busy

Little Miss
Quick

Little Miss
Wise

Little Miss
Tidy

Little Miss
Greedy

Little Miss
Fickle

Little Miss
Brainy

Little Miss
Stubborn

Little Miss
Curious

Little Miss
Fun

Little Miss
Contrary

Little Miss
Somersault

Little Miss
Scary

Little Miss
Bad

Little Miss
Whoops

Little Miss
Princess

Little Miss
Hug

Little Miss
Fabulous

Little Miss
Sparkle

$4.99 US
($6.99 CAN)

GROSSET&DUNLAP
Visit us at penguin.com/youngreaders
and mrmen.com

ISBN 978-0-8431-7426-7

EAN

9 780843 174267

50499 >